ZELLA
ZACK AND ZODIAC

Bill Peet

Houghton Mifflin Company

Boston

To
my brand-new
granddaughter
JENNIFER

Peet, Bill.
    Zella, Zack, and Zodiac.
    Summary: Zella the zebra helps Zack the ostrich
when he is young and helpless and when he grows up
Zack returns the favor by saving Zella's young
offspring from a lion.
    [1. Zebras—Fiction. 2. Ostriches—Fiction.
3. Friendship—Fiction. 4. Stories in rhyme]
I. Title.
PZ8.3.P2764Ze 1986   [E]   85-21991
ISBN 0-395-41069-X

Printed in the United States of America

Y 10 9 8 7 6 5 4 3 2

It was simply rotten luck that the little ostrich chick
Was born inside an eggshell that was just a bit too thick.
By the time he pecked his way out into broad daylight,
Everyone had gone. There was not a single soul in sight.
His mother had been frightened by a distant lion's roar
And departed with two other chicks just the night before.
"Whatever is to become of me?" the chick began to wonder,
When all at once there came a rumble, sounding just like thunder.

It was the thundering hoofbeats of an enormous zebra herd
That came galloping past by the thousands, a few yards from the bird.
"Help! Help! Help! Somebody!" the poor chick frantically cried.

"Please somebody! Help me! Won't somebody give me a ride?!"
But all of the zebras ignored him and kept on galloping past,
Until a young zebra named Zella took pity on him at last.

"You poor little thing!" exclaimed Zella. "Don't you have a mother, my dear?
What on earth are you doing all by yourself out here?"
"I'm brand new," replied the chick, "so how am I to know?
I just hatched out of my egg about half an hour ago."

"In this hot sun," warned the zebra, "you've got no chance at all to survive.
In another hour or two you'll surely be roasted alive.
So hop on my head, ostrich chick, then onto my back," said Zella.
"We'll go find you an acacia tree, they're like a big umbrella."

"There's not only lovely shade," said Zella, as they approached the tree,
"You'll find zillions of bugs to eat and live happily as can be.
But hold it! I smell danger!" she muttered, warily sniffing the air.
"It's a big cat! A leopard! He's crouched on a tree limb up there!"

Then in a twitch of a whisker, before the cat could attack,
Zella took off at a gallop with the chick clinging tight to her back.
Once they were safely in the clear and the zebra caught her breath,
She heaved a heavy sigh and said, "That cat nearly scared me to death!"
"I don't see why," the ostrich said, "he wasn't half your size.
I liked his beautiful spots and his big, bright yellow eyes."

"Now look here, chick," snorted Zella, becoming grumpy and stern,
"If you're so all-fired fearless then you've got a lot to learn.
You wouldn't last a minute if I dumped you on the ground.
There're too many dangerous beasts prowling all around.
There are lions and hyenas and then, for heaven sakes,
Roving packs of jackals and big, creeping, crawling snakes."

"If I'm stuck with you," sighed Zella, "as your foster mother,
I suppose that you should have a name of some kind or another.
Zachary is an old zebra name, I just now picked it out.
But I'd better call you just plain Zack in case I have to shout."

"Call me what you like," the ostrich chick replied.
"Zack is fine with me just as long as you'll let me ride."
"Then Zack it is!" cried Zella. "And now, my fearless bird,
Hang on tight while I turn on the speed to catch up with the herd."

The only time Zack was left on the ground was when it came time to feed.
Then the young ostrich raced through the weeds, darting about at top speed,
Snapping up snails and lizards and things ostriches like to eat,
But never straying very far from his zebra mother's feet.

"I've made up my mind," said Zack one day, "I'm going to stay on the ground.
I feel very silly at my age to be always carried around."
"You can do just as you like," snorted Zella. "Go out on your own, if you must.
But I'm afraid you'll feel even sillier if you get trampled into the dust."

"So I'll see you later!" Zack called out as he took off at a fast trot.
The foolhardy chick was going his way whether Zella liked it or not.
After that the zebra seldom saw her adopted ostrich son.
He was always racing about in the herd, always on the run.

And each time she caught a glimpse of Zack it was a big surprise.
It seemed to her that every few days he had almost doubled in size.
Her little chick was getting big and growing by leaps and bounds.
He was growing taller and taller and put on two hundred pounds.

And when Zack was nearly nine feet tall and all his growing was through,
He towered above the heads of the herd with a lofty bird's-eye view.
And he often trotted right past Zella without even saying hello,
But she supposed he couldn't see her since she was so far down below.

"Or is it possible," she wondered, "that Zack can't even remember
The horribly hot and miserable day a few years ago in September,
When he was a pitifully helpless chick crying out in despair,
Left all alone in the world, and without a mother to care?"

Late one afternoon as the herd stopped in a valley to graze,
And the sun had slipped away behind a pinkish-purple haze,
Zack came up to Zella to ask, "How are things going with you?
Are you getting along O.K. these days, and is there anything new?"

"You may have guessed," said Zella, "I'm expecting pretty soon.
That is why I resemble a big zebra-striped balloon.
I'll name the new one Zamantha if it should be a she,
Or he'll be called Zodiac if the colt should be a he."

21

Zella's new zebra, as it turned out, was a gawky, long-legged male,
Who seemed to be about perfect from the tip of his nose to his tail.
But one look at Zodiac's feet and Zella was suddenly frantic.
All four of the little colt's hoofs were nothing less than gigantic!

The new colt tottered about in an awkward attempt to trot,
But just a few staggering steps was as far as he ever got.
Then down went poor Zodiac, gigantic hoofs and all,
To end up on the ground in one clumsy headlong sprawl.

Then as he struggled to regain his feet, to Zella's great dismay,
A lion rose up from the grass a very short distance away.
Now this is what I call luck!" exclaimed the shaggy-maned beast,
"To happen upon a young zebra! What a fanciful feast!"
Panicky Zella's first thought was to cut loose and kick the big cat,
But she found she couldn't budge — she was too weak in the knees to do that.

All she could do was shout "Zodiac! Zodiac! Zodiac!
Watch out! There's a big lion! Watch out! He's about to attack!!"
Then as the lion leaped from the grass to pounce upon his prey,
All at once Zodiac took off and *WHOOSH!* went flying away.

Zack had come to the rescue without a split second to spare.
He had snatched the colt by the tail, then jerked him high in the air.

Then the brave and fearless ostrich took off and ran like a streak,
With Zella close on his heels and Zodiac's tail in his beak.

After the colt's close call with disaster, the ostrich made up his mind,
Wherever Zella and Zodiac went he'd always be close behind.

And Zack was ever so watchful, with his far-sighted ostrich eyes,
To make sure no lion or hyena could catch them by surprise.

Saving little Zodiac was one close call after another,
And a constant worry for his poor, jittery zebra mother.

If the colt's tail wasn't quite handy when a lion ventured too near,
Zack snatched him up by a hind leg or carried him off by an ear.
"How can I ever repay you?" grateful Zella asked one day.
"How can I ever thank you enough? What can I ever say?"

"Surely you must remember," the big ostrich winked and smiled,
"Once upon a time I was your troublesome problem child.
I wouldn't have lasted one day if it hadn't been for you.
Saving little Zodiac is the least that I can do.
And I'll keep on looking after him as long as I have a beak,
Until he grows up to fit his feet and can gallop like a streak."